P9-EMQ-693

Mr. Bumble

Kim Kennedy
Illustrated by Doug Kennedy

Hyperion Books for Children
New York

Every spring, the meadows became a buzzing and busy scene,
with hundreds of bumblebees gathering pollen for their hive.

Such work came easily to all the bees.

To all, that is, but one.

His name was Mr. Bumble, and he was the clumsiest bee who ever buzzed. Sadly, when it came to gathering pollen, he could never take off from a flower without bumbling, fumbling, and tumbling.

While the other bees buzzed back to their queen with mounds of the golden dust, Mr. Bumble always returned with the smallest share. "Another empty bucket!" Queen Bee would fuss. "Dents are all *you* seem to gather!"

One evening, the queen held court. "Something grand has happened!"
she announced. "Today, one of our scouts buzzed over an undiscovered
clover patch! There you will find a gold mine of pollen!"

Everyone was excited about the news, except Mr. Bumble. He couldn't help wondering what might lurk in that patch, just waiting to catch a clumsy bee.

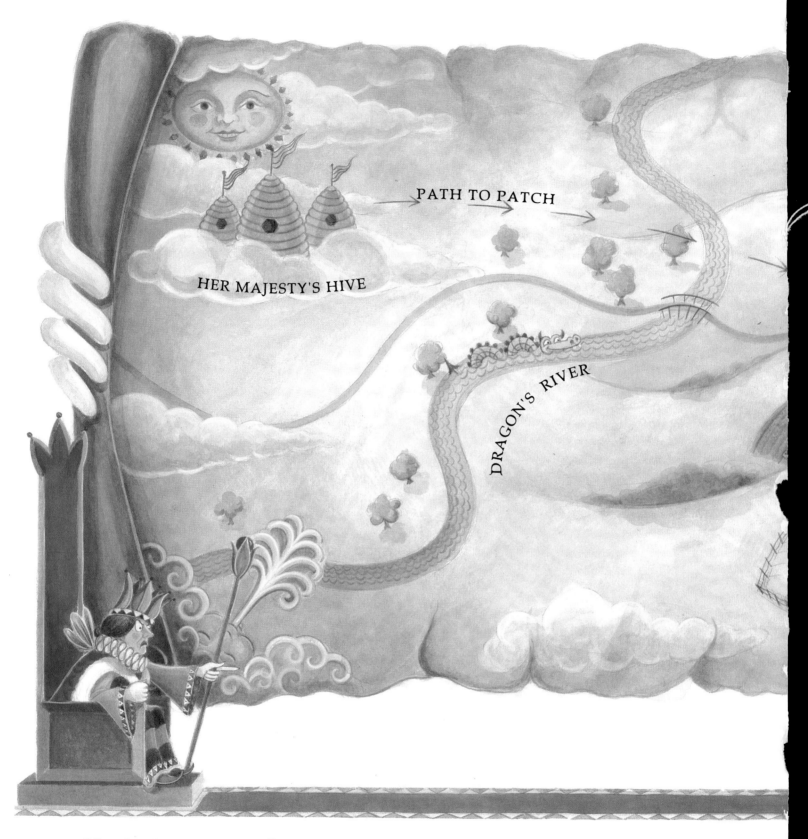

"Study this map well!" declared the queen, "for tomorrow you journey there."

"But what *else* did the scout see?" Mr. Bumble asked. "Does something *live* in that patch? And if so, what if it's *mean*?"

THE DARK FOREST

DAIRY FARM

THE CLOVER PATCH

"Well," said the queen, "if that's true, those of you who are quick and clever have nothing to fear. But those who are *not*," she added, looking at Mr. Bumble, "**Beware!**"

To Mr. Bumble, things looked grim indeed. For even if he made it to the patch, he could only guess what terrible things awaited him there. That night he dreamed of monsters doing dreadful deeds, like plucking out his very wings!

Though the next morning's journey was long and hard,
Mr. Bumble finally managed to arrive, but only to find
that the other bees had already filled their buckets and
flown away.

Teetering atop a blossom, Mr. Bumble began his lonely
work. *Plink* went the pollen into his bucket. *Clink* went
some more. But just as he was going *plinkety clink* to
the next flower, a frightful noise arose that sent a shiver round
his stripes and curled his little toes.

Mr. Bumble had to get out of there and get out of there quick. But he tripped and stumbled and landed with a horrible crash!

"Oh, no!" he yelped in a helpless heap. "I'm done for!" he cried in fear, for not only was he seeing stars but the bucket was stuck on his head.

Suddenly, he was hoisted high in the air. "Please let me go!" Mr. Bumble squeaked. Yet higher still he went. "Don't pluck out my wings!" he begged.

"Why ever would we do that?" came a tiny voice as he was set gently upon the ground. Then the bucket was lifted away, revealing a splendid sight.

"Fairies!" he buzzed with relief. Looking about, he realized how wrong he had been. Indeed, there wasn't one monster in the entire clover patch.

As for the lift the fairies gave him, it was the best flight he'd ever had. "If I could fly like a fairy," he sighed, "I could gather pollen as well as the other bees."

"We can teach you," the fairies chimed. "We'll show you how it's done."

Swirl

Figure Eight

Mr. Bumble's first lesson was in taking off, so they launched him from a tiny bluebonnet. Beneath him they stretched a spiderweb net to catch him if he fell.

With a **boing** and a **buzzzz** he sailed into the air, flying higher and straighter with each and every try. And when Mr. Bumble took off without trouble, the fairies knew it was time for his next lesson: how to land gently upon a flower.

They guided Mr. Bumble by daisy chains so he wouldn't belly flop. He learned to step upon flowers without disturbing a single raindrop.

How To Land

For the first time, he buzzed without bumbling,
flew without fumbling, and twirled without tumbling.
"I can finally fly with grace!" he cried.

This called for a celebration!
So the fairies held a flying party for Mr. Bumble,
where he could give all their tricks a whirl. And
never before had the sky been filled with such fancy
feats of flight.

Soon it was time for Mr. Bumble to go, so he filled his
bucket with pollen. "Thank you, my friends," he buzzed
as they all waved good-bye. And with his bucket held
high, off he flew to his hive.

Meanwhile, the queen was searching the evening sky. "That clumsy Mr. Bumble must be lost again," she sighed. Just then, she spotted a bee zipping through the air. "Surely that can't be **Mr. Bumble** buzzing there."

But who was it but Mr. Bumble who glided all the way to her throne.
"For Her Royal Highness," he said. And with a buzz and a bow, he
presented his astonished queen with his bucket of golden dust.

"Hurrah!" cheered his fellow bees. Why, the queen cheered for him, too. "What a fine bee you turned out to be!" she said. "You deserve something better to carry."

With that, she presented Mr. Bumble with a bucket made of gold.

As for Mr. Bumble's old bucket, it was placed for future bees to see. "Though old and worn," said Queen Bee, "it is still an inspiring sight. Look on it as the humble beginning to every perfect flight."

To our family and Opal and Paul Bauer

To Shannon Murphy
—K. K.

To Matt Robinson
—D. K.

Text © 1997 by Kim Kennedy. Illustrations © 1997 by Doug Kennedy. · All rights reserved. No part of this book may be reproduced or transmitted in any form or by any means, electronic or mechanical, including photocopying, recording, or by any information storage and retrieval system, without written permission from the publisher. For information address Hyperion Books for Children, 114 Fifth Avenue, New York, New York 10011-5690. · Printed in the United States of America. · First Edition   3 5 7 9 10 8 6 4   · The artwork for each picture is prepared using acrylic on paper. · This book is set in 20-point OPTIEve-Light. · Library of Congress Cataloging-in-Publication Data. Kennedy, Kim. Mr. Bumble / Kim Kennedy ; illustrated by Doug Kennedy. — 1st ed.   p.   cm. Summary: Mr. Bumble, the clumsiest bee in his hive, learns how to gather pollen gracefully and efficiently from a group of helpful fairies. ISBN 0-7868-0263-4 (trade)—ISBN 0-7868-2293-7 (lib. bdg.) [1. Bees—Fiction. 2. Fairies—Fiction. 3. Stories in rhyme.] I. Kennedy, Doug, ill. II. Title. PZ8.3.K38325Mj   1997 [E]—dc21 96-35465